Ooh,

stop.

With your feet on the air
and your head on the ground

Try this trick
and spin it,

yeah

Your head will
collapse

But there's
nothing in it

And you'll ask
yourself

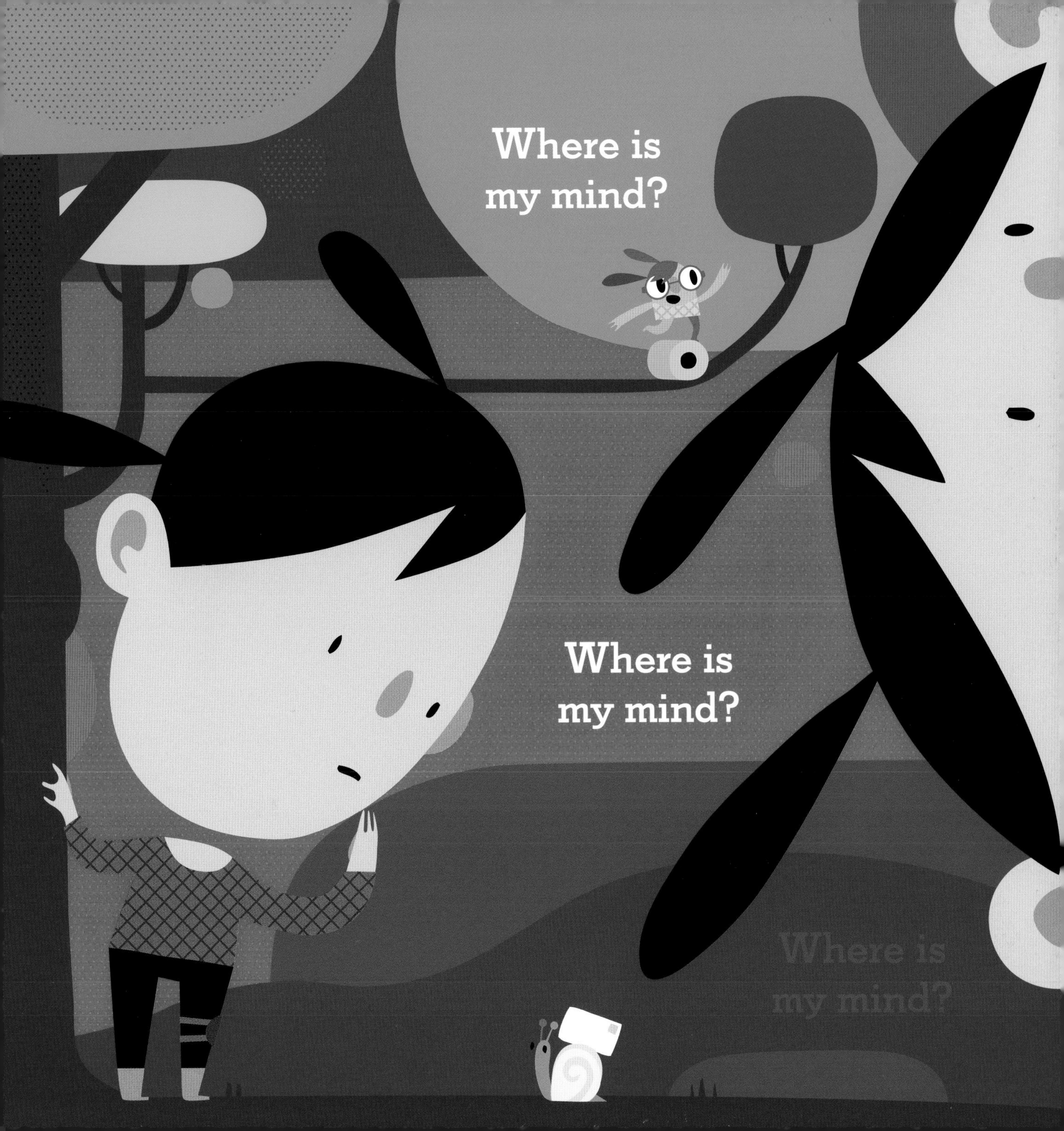

Where is
my mind?

Where is
my mind?

Where is
my mind?

Way out
in the water

See it swimmin'

I was swimmin' in
the Caribbean

Animals were hiding
behind the rock

Except the little fish
bumped into me

I swear he was tryin'
to talk to me

coy koi

Way out
in the water

See it swimmin'

With your feet on the air and your head on the ground

Try this trick
and spin it,

yeah

Your head will collapse
If there's nothing in it

And you'll ask
yourself

Where is
my mind?

Way out
in the water

See it swimmin'

ooh

With your feet on the air
and your head on the ground

Try this trick and spin it,

yeah

LOOK OUT FOR THESE LyricPop TITLES

The 59th Street Bridge Song (Feelin' Groovy)
SONG LYRICS BY PAUL SIMON • ILLUSTRATIONS BY KEITH HENRY BROWN

Paul Simon's groovy anthem to New York City provides a joyful basis for this live-for-the-day picture book.

African
SONG LYRICS BY PETER TOSH • ILLUSTRATIONS BY RACHEL MOSS

A beautiful children's picture book featuring the lyrics of Peter Tosh's global classic celebrating people of African descent.

(Sittin' on) The Dock of the Bay
SONG LYRICS BY OTIS REDDING AND STEVE CROPPER • IILLUSTRATIONS BY KAITLYN SHEA O'CONNOR

Otis Redding and Steve Cropper's timeless ode to never-ending days is given fresh new life in this heartwarming picture book.

Don't Stop
SONG LYRICS BY CHRISTINE McVIE • ILLUSTRATIONS BY NUSHA ASHJAEE

Christine McVie's classic song for Fleetwood Mac about keeping one's chin up and rolling with life's punches is beautifully adapted to an uplifting children's book.

Dream Weaver
SONG LYRICS BY GARY WRIGHT • ILLUSTRATIONS BY ROB SAYEGH JR.

Gary Wright's hit song is reimagined as a fantastical picture book to delight dreamers of all ages.

Good Vibrations
SONG LYRICS BY MIKE LOVE AND BRIAN WILSON • ILLUSTRATIONS BY PAUL HOPPE

Mike Love and Brian Wilson's world-famous song for the Beach Boys, gloriously illustrated by Paul Hoppe, will bring smiles to the faces of children and parents alike.

Humble and Kind
SONG LYRICS BY LORI McKENNA • ILLUSTRATIONS BY KATHERINE BLACKMORE

Award-winning songwriter Lori McKenna's iconic song—as popularized by Tim McGraw—is the perfect basis for a picture book that celebrates family and togetherness.